The Inside-Outside

Book of New

York City

The Inside-Outside

Book of New York City

ROXIE MUNRO

SEASTAR BOOKS • NEW YORK

SEASTAR BOOKS • A division of NORTH-SOUTH BOOKS INC.
Published in the United States by SeaStar Books, a division of North-South Books Inc., New York.
Published simultaneously in Canada, Australia, and New Zealand by North-South Books, an imprint of Nord-Süd Verlag AG, Gossau Zürich, Switzerland.

Library of Congress Cataloging-in-Publication Data is available.
The artwork for this book was prepared by using watercolors.
1 2 3 4 5 6 7 8 9 10 RT • ISBN 1-58717-081-7 (reinforced trade binding)
1 2 3 4 5 6 7 8 9 10 PB • ISBN 1-58717-082-5 (paperback binding)
Printed by Proost NV in Belgium
For more information about our books, and the authors and artists who create them, visit our web site: www.northsouth.com

TO MY MOTHER AND FATHER, AND TO BO

The Flatiron Building

The American Museum of Natural History

The Statue of Liberty

The New York Stock Exchange

Subway at Times Square

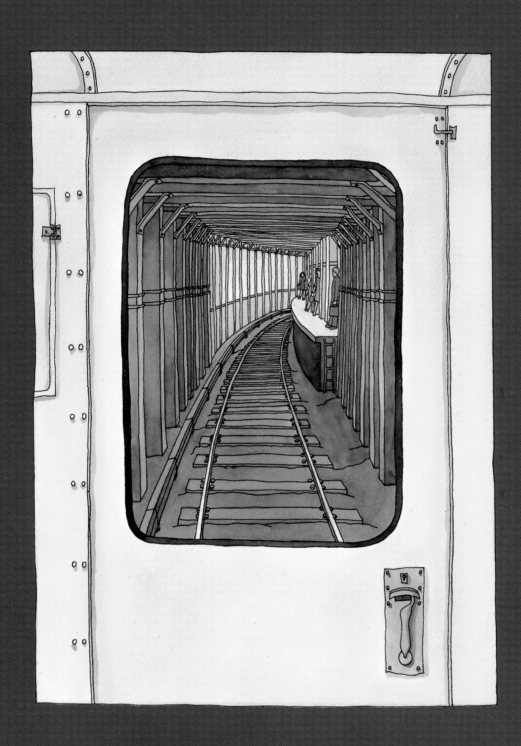

Madison Square Garden

Avenue of the Americas at 19th Street

New York Zoological Park (The Bronx Zoo)

New York State Theater at Lincoln Center

St. Patrick's Cathedral

CHRYSLER BUILDING (cover) Between 42nd and 43rd Streets on Lexington Avenue, this 77-story building was the first structure to top the Eiffel Tower in height. Built in 1930, its classic Art Deco geometric style is a culmination of the skyscraper building boom of the 1920s. The view is from the 71st floor in the spire.

EMPIRE STATE BUILDING (title pages) Standing 1,472 feet high at 350 Fifth Avenue and built in 1931, this was the tallest building in the world until 1974, when the World Trade Center went up. Each year, 3.8 million people enjoy spectacular views from the 86th- (shown in art) and 102nd-floor observatories. Visibility extends to 80 miles in clear weather. There are 7 miles of elevator shafts, 1,860 steps to floor 102, and 6,500 windows to wash twice a month. Observatories are open every day.

FLATIRON BUILDING In 1902, when it went up on the triangular site where Fifth Avenue joins Broadway at 23rd Street, many New Yorkers thought this 21-story building would topple over in the first strong wind. The limestone façade is just decoration, however; this was one of the first skyscrapers to be supported with a steel framework. Art shows the view from offices on the 16th floor, looking north.

AMERICAN MUSEUM OF NATURAL HISTORY Built in various stages from 1877 on, the museum sprawls between Central Park West and Columbus Avenue from 77th to 81st Streets. Almost 12 acres of space house 35 million artifacts and specimens, including the world's largest dinosaur collection, the largest meteorite ever retrieved in the United States, the Star of India sapphire, and more fossil mammals than can be found in any other museum in the world. Art shows the façade of the Theodore Roosevelt Memorial Wing and Carl Akeley African Mammals Hall. Open every day.

STATUE OF LIBERTY Originally known as "Liberty Enlightening the World," this colossal torchbearer was a gift from the people of France to the people of the United States. Designed by Frederic August Bartholdi and reinforced in iron by Gustave Eiffel, she was erected in a Paris studio, dismantled into 350 pieces, and packed in 210 crates. Nine years later, U.S. citizens raised enough money to erect the statue on what is now Liberty Island in New York Harbor. It was dedicated on October 28, 1886. Her index finger is 8 feet long, her mouth is 3 feet wide, and her skin is made of copper sheets 3/32 of an inch thick.

NEW YORK STOCK EXCHANGE An average of one billion shares of stock are traded each day on the world's largest exchange, located at 8 Broad Street. From the visitors' gallery, one may view the organized chaos of the "floor." Tours explain the complexities of buying and selling as well as the use of computers, the roles of the brokers and of the people in various colored jackets (floor supervisors, messengers, reporters who transmit trading information to computers and ticker tapes, and other employees). The ceiling network of yellow tubes encloses the complex electrical circuitry necessary to support and air-condition this hothouse of capitalist activity.

SUBWAY AT TIMES SQUARE Approximately four million people daily ride 656 miles of subway track in the five boroughs of New York City. The Times Square Station is the busiest. The green globe lights mean the token booth is open 24 hours a day. Times Square is famous for its theaters, restaurants, nightlife, and glittering neon signage.

MADISON SQUARE GARDEN After two previous locations, the present garden, built in 1968 between Seventh and Eighth Avenues and 31st and 33rd Streets, is home to the New York Knickerbockers ("Knicks") basketball team and the New York Rangers hockey team. It hosts numerous sporting events and shows, including the Ringling Bros. and Barnum & Bailey Circus.

AVENUE OF THE AMERICAS AT 19th STREET Known as "Ladies' Mile" at the turn of the twentieth century because of the fashionable department stores along the avenue, this area combines business, fashion, art, photography, theater, and residential living. Sixth Avenue, renamed Avenue of the Americas in 1945 as a part of the U.S. Good Neighbor policy, acquired its bike lane (of which there are 138 miles in the five boroughs) in 1978.

NEW YORK ZOOLOGICAL PARK The largest urban zoo in the nation opened in 1899 at its present location at Fordham Road and the Bronx River Parkway. Approximately 3,600 animals, many roaming free, are displayed in over 265 acres. The zoo is a leader in propagating endangered species and has a "hands on" children's zoo where special exhibits also allow youngsters to explore animal habitats, locomotion, and defenses. The art depicts the DeJur Aviary, the home of South American sea birds. Open every day.

NEW YORK STATE THEATER Built between 1962 and 1966 at 64th and Broadway, Lincoln Center includes the Metropolitan Opera House, Avery Fisher Hall, the Library and Museum of the Performing Arts, the Vivian Beaumont Theater, the Juilliard School of Music, as well as the New York State Theater, home to the New York City Ballet and New York City Opera. The art shows a scene from the second act of *The Nutcracker*, presented each December by NYCB. (Music by Peter Ilyitch Tchaikovsky, Choreography by George Balanchine, Scenery and Lighting by Rouben Ter-Arutunian, and Costumes by Karinska.)

ST. PATRICK'S CATHEDRAL Its spires soaring to 330 feet above Fifth Avenue between 50th and 51st Streets, the cathedral is the seat of the Roman Catholic Archdiocese. It was built between 1878 and 1888, influenced by the cathedrals of Rheims and Cologne. The huge nave, seating about 2,500, is open every day to people of all faiths. Suspended from the ceiling vault are the red hats of the first four Cardinal Archbishops of New York.

DATE DUE

MAR 2 9 2003	
MAY 2 7 2003	
JUN 1 1 2003	
DEC 1 4 2004	
APR 1 8 2005	
AUG 1 7 2005	
JUL 2 0 2006	
APR 1 5 2008	
JUL 2 8 2008	

BRODART, CO.   Cat. No. 23-221-003